Oxford University Press, Walton Street, Oxford OX2 6DP

OXFORD LONDON GLASGOW
NEW YORK TORONTO MELBOURNE WELLINGTON
KUALA LUMPUR SINGAPORE HONG KONG TOKYO
DELHI BOMBAY CALCUTTA MADRAS KARACHI
NAIROBI DAR ES SALAAM CAPE TOWN

© *Victor G. Ambrus, 1980*

ISBN 0 19 279727 1

Printed in Great Britain by
W. S. Cowell Ltd. at the Butter Market, Ipswich

24348

The Valiant
Little Tailor
Victor G. Ambrus

Oxford New York Toronto Melbourne
OXFORD UNIVERSITY PRESS · 1980

One fine summer morning a tailor was sitting sewing at a
waistcoat when along the street came a farmer's wife, shouting

'Tasty home-made jam, tasty home-made jam for sale'. This
sounded nice to the tailor, so out he came, saying 'Your jam

sounds so good I'll buy half a jar.' The farmer's wife, who hoped to sell more, went away grumbling, and the tailor took his jam inside.

'This jam will give me enough energy to finish the waistcoat,' thought the tailor happily, spreading a slice of bread thickly with jam, 'but I'll just finish sewing on these buttons.'

The smell of the jam rose to the ceiling, and a large number of flies began to swarm around. 'Who asked *you* to a picnic,' shouted the tailor, flinging up his arms at them. In a fury he grabbed a roll of cloth and brought it down sharply on the table.

When he lifted it up, he discovered no less than seven flies lying dead with outstretched legs. 'How brave I am,' he said to himself, admiring his deed, 'the whole town shall know of this.' With that, he cut himself a broad belt, embroidering it in large letters with 'Seven With One Blow', and fastened it around his waist. But so proud did he feel that he determined not just the town but the whole world should know of his courage. So he set off, taking with him a large round cheese in a cloth, and popping his pet canary into his pocket to keep him company on the journey.

Outside the town on a hill there lived a Giant who used to terrify the inhabitants on market day by carrying away all the cows and sheep he could lay hands on, smashing everything in his way. The little tailor's road led him up the hill, and at the top he found the Giant sitting there, looking at the world below him.

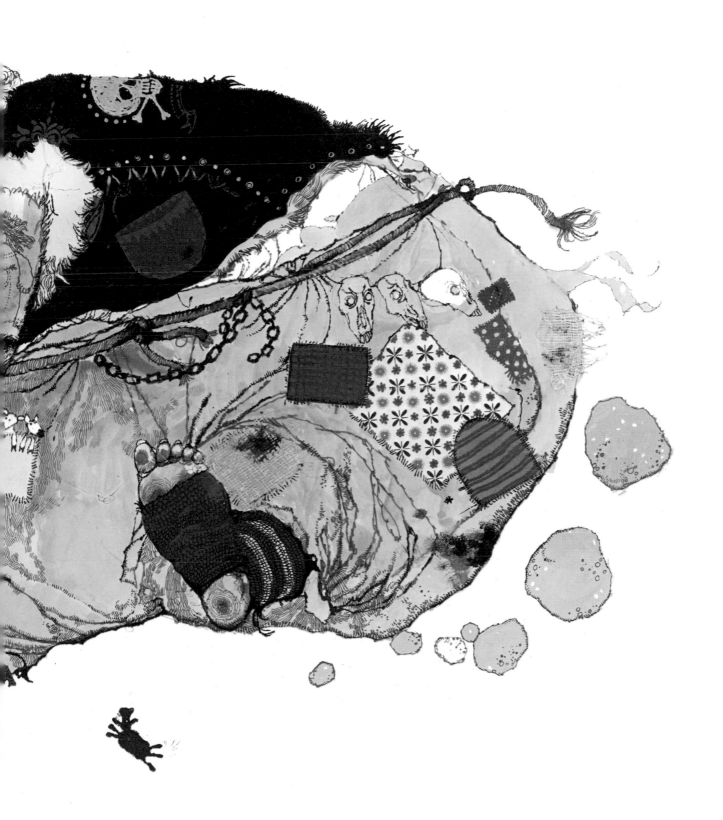

The tailor walked boldly up to him and gave him a prod with his stick. 'Good day my friend,' he said, 'don't just sit there. I am on my way to try my luck in the world – you may join me if you wish.' The Giant looked at him with contempt. 'You miserable little fellow, how dare you talk to me like that?' 'I may be little,' said the tailor, 'but read what kind of man I am on this belt!' 'Seven With One Blow', read the Giant, becoming a little uneasy.

'Let's see how strong you are,' roared the Giant, and picked up a large stone. 'Do this after me!' he shouted, and squeezed the stone so hard that water dripped from it.

'That's child's play to me,' said the little
tailor. He unwrapped his round cheese
and squeezed it until all the juice ran
out. The Giant hardly knew what to say.
He picked up a large rock and threw it
so high it could scarcely be seen.
'There manikin!' he roared, 'Do that
after me!' 'Good try,' said the tailor, 'but
your stone fell to the ground. I will
throw one up that won't come down.'
With that he pulled the canary from his
pocket and threw it up in the air. The
bird flew straight up and away, never to
return.

'You can certainly throw well,' admitted the Giant, 'but let's see if you can help me carry this tree.'

'Why just one tree, why not the whole forest?' asked the little tailor cheekily. 'Just get hold of the trunk and I shall carry the end with the branches, which is heavier.' The Giant took up the tree and staggered away under its weight while the tailor hopped on a branch behind so that the Giant could not see him. There

he sat, singing away as if carrying a tree was also child's play. The Giant became so exhausted that he could go no further and put the tree down. The tailor jumped off just in time and put his arms around the tree as if he had been carrying it all the time, saying, 'You are such a big fellow, yet you can't carry this tree by yourself?'

'Since you are such a valiant little fellow, come with me and be my guest for the night,' said the Giant, by now impressed.

The tailor accepted the invitation and entered the Giant's cave where a second Giant sat by the fire, with a roast sheep in each hand. 'This certainly is more interesting than my old workshop,' thought the tailor, making himself comfortable in a huge bed the Giant showed him. After a while the little tailor found this bed uncomfortable and rather too big, so he slipped out of it and went to sleep on a rug in the corner.

At midnight, when the Giant thought the tailor was fast asleep, he got up and hit the bed with a huge iron bar, so hard that he cut right through it. Thinking that was the end of the tailor, the two Giants got up early and went into the forest to look for lost sheep. Suddenly they came upon the tailor singing away merrily, picking flowers in a field. The Giants were terrified and ran away so fast that the whole forest shook under them.

The tailor journeyed on happily until he found himself in the gardens of what looked like a Royal Palace. By this time he was rather tired, so he lay down on the lawn and soon fell asleep.

As he lay there many people passed by and read on his belt 'Seven With One Blow'. 'What a great warrior this traveller must be!' they said, and called the Princess to come and read the belt for herself. 'This must be some mighty hero,' thought the pretty Princess, and at once fell in love with the little tailor. She ran and told the King that a mighty warrior lay asleep in the Palace gardens. The King sent one of his courtiers to await the tailor's awakening and invite him into the Royal service. 'It would be a pleasure!' said the little tailor when he woke up, and followed the courtier to the King.

'In the forest in my kingdom live two Giants,' said the King. 'By robbery and murder they create great havoc, and no man dares to approach them without risking his life. If you can overcome these Giants I will give you my daughter's hand in marriage, and half my kingdom. A hundred soldiers of my best regiments shall

accompany you.' 'That will not be necessary,' said the little
tailor. 'I'd rather fight these villains by myself. A man who kills
seven with one blow need not fear *two!*' The tailor then set off
into the forest, but first filled his coat pockets with stones. Soon
he could hear the two Giants snoring under a large tree. He
clambered up above them and dropped a stone onto the chest of
one of the Giants. The Giant stopped snoring, and gave the other
a shove with his elbow. 'What are you
hitting me for?' he asked.

'Go to sleep. I never hit you!' said the other, and they both
started snoring all over again. The tailor dropped a stone on the
second Giant. 'What's this?!' he shouted, 'What are you hitting
me for?'
'You must be dreaming' replied the first Giant and again they

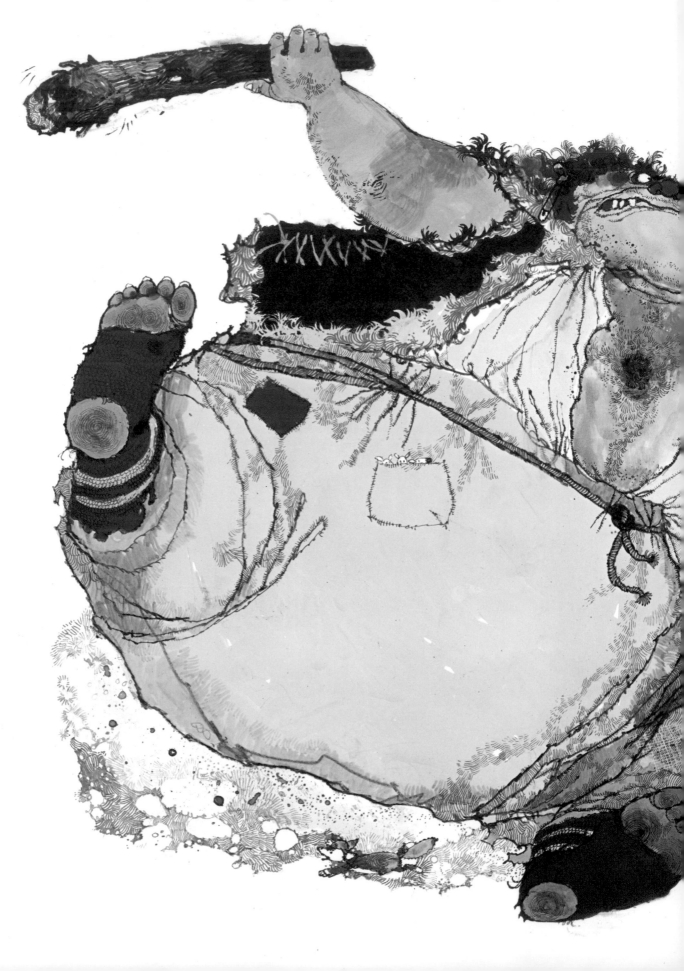

went to sleep. Then the little tailor picked out his largest stone and hit the first Giant right on the nose.

'This is too bad!' the Giant shouted in a rage, and hit his friend who was just as angry and hit back with all his strength. They uprooted several trees and beat one another so hard that they fell senseless to the ground!

Now the tailor quickly jumped down and tied them up with a huge rope.

By the time the King and his soldiers arrived the little tailor was standing on top of the Giants with his sword drawn, as if he had just finished fighting them. The King could hardly believe his eyes! He was so delighted that he immediately organized a splendid wedding celebration, and gave the tailor half his kingdom as a wedding present. The Princess and the little tailor were very happy together, but then the King's jealous courtiers overheard the little tailor talking in his sleep, saying, 'Boy, make me a waistcoat, stitch up those trousers, or I shall lay a yardstick across your bottom!' They rushed to the King and told him that his brave son-in-law was nothing but a jumped-up tailor. The King was very annoyed by this and decided to listen to the tailor himself, ready with his servants to tie him up and carry him off to the dungeons. When the Princess heard of her father's plans, she told everything to her beloved little tailor.

When night came the tailor pretended to snore for a while, and then began to shout in a loud voice, 'Boy, make me a waistcoat, stitch up those trousers, or I shall lay a yardstick across your bottom. Seven have I killed with one blow, two Giants have I slain, and now I am about to finish off all those outside my door!' With a great shout he jumped out of bed and drew his sword. Away ran the King and his servants, and no man ever dared to oppose the little tailor again. In time he became a very wise King, but he did have two weaknesses: he always made his own waistcoats, and he was very fond of home-made jam!